DINNER with the DODOS

ADAPTED BY LESLIE GOLDMAN

HarperEntertainment
An Imprint of HarperCollins*Publishers*

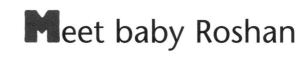

Meet baby Roshan

and his funny new friends

Manny, Sid, and Diego.

These new buddies
are taking Roshan back
to his family.

But they have a long
journey ahead—

a VERY long journey. . . .

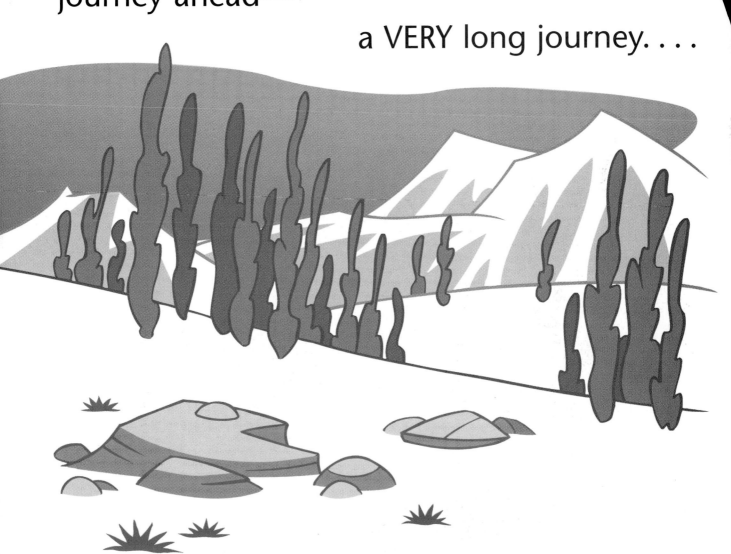

After a while, Roshan fell asleep.

When he woke up, he started to cry.

At first no one knew why.

"I'll make him stop," said Diego.

He covered his eyes and purred, "Where's the baby?"

"There he is!"

"I bet he's hungry," said Sid.

"How about some milk?" asked Manny.

"I'd love some!" Sid licked his lips.

Just then, Manny spotted a big melon on the ground.

He was sure their
worries were over.

Manny picked up the melon, but in a flash a dodo bird named Dab ran by.

Dab took the melon
from Manny's trunk!

Manny, Sid, Diego, and
Roshan followed Dab to
the dodos' camp. Dab
had three melons.

"Guys, can we have our melon back?" Manny asked.

"No way!" said Dab.

Then Dab tripped on the melon. It flew into the air—right to Roshan!

"Oh, no! Get that melon!" yelled Dab.

"Tae kwon dodos, attack!" he called to his friends.

Meanwhile, another
dodo grabbed the melon.

He threw it to the
dodo behind him,

who threw it to the
dodo behind him.

Then the last dodo in
line threw the melon
over a cliff.

But Sid wasn't worried.
There were still two
tasty melons to eat.

Sid took one, but the
dodos grabbed it back.
But they lost that
melon, too.

Only one melon was
left. The dodos ran
after it.

They jumped on it. It
went shooting up into
the sky.

Sid raced after it
just as fast as he could.

And he caught it!

"Put the melon down!" yelled a dodo in a very loud voice.

Sid held on to that melon as if it were the last one on earth.

He dodged dodos, right and left.

He ran all the way to Diego, Manny, and Roshan.

Sid was so happy, he did a little dance.

Then he slammed the melon to the ground. It splattered everywhere.

"Great, now we've got to find more food!" yelled Diego.

But Roshan didn't mind at all. The melon was just the right size for him.